Let's go Shopping Peppa

Once upon a time, Peppa and George were having their breakfast.
"What are we doing today, Daddy?" asked Peppa.
"We need to go shopping," replied Daddy Pig, rubbing
his tummy. "For lunch!"

"Yippee!" cheered Peppa and George.
They loved going shopping.

This book belongs to

....

LADYBIRD BOOKS

UK | USA | Canada | Ireland | Australia
India | New Zealand | South Africa

Ladybird Books is part of the Penguin Random House group of companies
whose addresses can be found at global.penguinrandomhouse.com.

www.penguin.co.uk   www.puffin.co.uk   www.ladybird.co.uk

 Penguin
Random House
UK

First published 2015
This edition 2016
001

Printed in China

ISBN: 978-0-241-26880-3

Toot!
Toot!

When breakfast was finished,
everyone jumped into the car.

"We're here!" cheered Peppa when they arrived at the supermarket.
Peppa and George leapt out of the car and started jumping up and down excitedly.
They loved the supermarket!
"First, we need a trolley," said Peppa.

Daddy Pig put George in the trolley.
"Snort! Snort!" said George happily.
"Daddy," said Peppa, "can I sit in the trolley, too?"

"Ho! Ho!" laughed Daddy Pig.
"You're too big, Peppa.
But you can help
with the shopping."

"Oh, goody," said Peppa, skipping into the supermarket.

There was so much to see inside.

"Can we get one of **everything**?" asked Peppa.

"No, Peppa, that would be far too much," replied Mummy Pig.

"But how do we know what to get?" asked Peppa.

"We use this," said Daddy Pig,
holding up a piece of paper.
"Oooh," said Peppa.
"What's **that**?"

4 tomatoes
Spaghetti
4 onions
Fruit

"It's our shopping list," explained
Mummy Pig. "We have four things
on our list."

Daddy Pig looked at the list closely and read it out slowly.
"Four tomatoes . . . spaghetti . . . four onions . . . fruit."

4 tomatoes

Spaghetti

4 onions

Fruit

"I'll find it all!" said Peppa.

"I can see the tomatoes!" cried Peppa.

Peppa counted four tomatoes as Mummy Pig put them into a bag: "One, two, three, four." She skipped off to put them in the trolley. Daddy Pig crossed them off the list.

4 tomatoes

"What's next on the list?"
asked Mummy Pig.
"Can you remember?"

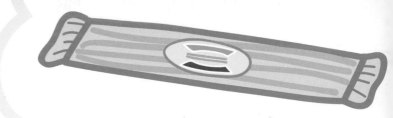

"Spaghetti!"
cheered Peppa.

"Pee-getty!"
cheered George.

Spaghetti was Peppa and George's favourite.
"I can see it!" cried Peppa. "Follow me."

Peppa found the spaghetti,
and put it in the trolley.
"Well done, Peppa,"
said Mummy Pig.

Peppa and George couldn't remember
what was next on the list.

"Dine-saw?" guessed George.
"George," said Peppa, "there aren't
any dinosaurs in the supermarket."

Daddy Pig laughed. "Onions are next."

"Onions!" cried Peppa. "I remember."
She raced off and counted four onions into a bag:

"One,   two,   three,   four."
Then she put them in the trolley.

"Well done, Peppa,"
said Daddy Pig, crossing them off the list.

4 tomatoes

Spaghetti

4 onions

The last thing on the list was fruit.
"I'll get it!" cried Peppa.
"It's George's turn now," said Mummy Pig.

"Snort! Snort!"
replied George.

"How about
bananas?"
suggested Peppa.

"Or apples . . .
Or pears . . .

Or oranges?"

George shook his head.
He didn't want any of Peppa's
suggestions. He wanted
a **very big** . . .

...watermelon!

"Grunt! Grunt!" George was very happy
with his choice, even though it was bigger than him!
Daddy Pig passed George the watermelon.
It was very heavy!

George dropped the watermelon in the trolley.
Rattle! Rattle! It was so big the whole trolley shook!

"Hee! Hee! Hee!"

Everyone laughed.
"Well done, George."

Daddy Pig crossed fruit off the shopping list.
"That's everything," said Mummy Pig.
"Let's head to the checkout and pay."

At the checkout, Peppa and Daddy Pig put the food
on the conveyor belt. Miss Rabbit scanned each thing.

"Tomatoes."   "Onions."   "Watermelon."   "Spaghetti."

BEEP!   BEEP!   BEEP!   BEEP!

"Great big chocolate cake." BEEP!

"Chocolate cake?" said Mummy Pig, Peppa
and George. "That wasn't on the list."

"Peppa, did you put a chocolate cake in the trolley?"
asked Mummy Pig.
"No, Mummy," replied Peppa.
"George, did you put a chocolate cake in the trolley?"
asked Mummy Pig.
"No," replied George.
"Well, I didn't put it in the trolley," said Mummy Pig.

"Then who did?"
asked Peppa.

"Er," said Daddy Pig, holding up the chocolate cake guiltily. "I thought it might be nice for pudding."
"Daddy Pig!" said Mummy Pig.
"Sorry!" said Daddy Pig, turning red.
"It just looked so delicious. Snort!"
"It does look rather yummy," said Mummy Pig.
"Let's pretend it was on the list."

"Hooray!" everyone cheered.

When Peppa and her family arrived home, it was time for lunch. They had delicious spaghetti, followed by a big piece of watermelon and a great big slice of chocolate cake!

Peppa, George, Mummy Pig and Daddy Pig loved going shopping for food, but they loved eating it most of all!